Lake

Lake Stories of Wales

Shadows in the Waters

by

Margaret Isaac

Illustrations by
Margaret Jones

APECS PRESS CAERLEON

Published by
APECS Press
Caerleon
Wales UK

© Margaret Isaac 2008

Editing and design by
APECS Press Caerleon

ISBN 978 0 9548940 6 1

*All rights reserved.
No part of this work may be reproduced or stored
in an information retrieval system
(other than short excerpts for purposes of review)
without the express permission of the Publishers given in writing.*

Margaret Isaac has asserted her right
under the Copyright, Design and Patents Act 1988
to be identified as author of this work.

Printed in Wales by Gwasg Dinefwr Llandybie

Contents

Foreword vii

Acknowledgements ix

The Mystery of Llyn Cwm Llwch 1

Llyn Safaddon: Where No Birds Sing 13

Kenfig Pool: The Curse of the Pantannas 23

Llyn Llech Owain: Arthur's Greatest Knight 39

The Lady of Llyn-y-Fan Fach 61

By the same author

Tales of Gold: Stories of Caves, Gold and Magic

Nia and the Magic of the Lake: The story of a growing friendship between a boy and a girl set against the backdrop of the legend of Llyn-y-Fan Fach.

Sir Gawain and the Green Knight: It is Christmas time in King Arthur's court. Gawain, Arthur's nephew, accepts a mortal challenge from an enchanted giant.

Rhiannon's Way: Caradog, a Celtic Chieftain, has been captured by the Romans. His daughter Rhiannon sets out to rescue him with the help of her friend Brychan and a little help from a magic pony and a magic mirror.

The Tale of Twm Siôn Cati: The story of how a Welshman resisted the oppression of Tudor times on behalf of the poor in the same way as another Celtic hero, the Scottish outlaw, Rob Roy.

Language Resources for Schools: Based upon and complementary to the books of fiction referred to above.

Forthcoming publications

Thomas Jones alias Twm Siôn Cati: Events in the life of Thomas Jones after his reprieve from Elizabeth I for his outlaw days as Twm Siôn Cati.

Lake Stories of Wales: Book Two.

Foreword

VISITING THE Welsh Lakes is a joy. You will find corries, like the sinister Lake Glaslyn, large lakes like the serene Llyn Safaddon, small lakes, hanging on the side of the mountain, like the forbidding Llydaw, hidden beneath the mountain face, like the endearing Llyn Cwm Llwch, or tucked away beneath the Black Mountain like the entrancing Llyn-y-Fan Fach.

The lakes of Wales are different in size, shape, vegetation and location and are constantly changing, due to weather, climate, time and human interference. These things make them unforgettable, what makes them unique are the stories. Stories of enchantment, of knights in armour, lost treasure, spirits of the underworld, monsters lurking beneath the waters, drowned villages, and lost cultures.

I have enjoyed immensely visiting the lakes, and talking to local people. I have been inspired by the great authorities on Wales and the Celtic world, writers like Sir John Rhys, Gwynfor Evans, Hywel Dda and Gerald of Wales. The writer to whom I was first indebted for my initial exploration into the world of the Welsh Lakes was a respected fisherman, Frank Ward. His book guided me to the locations and began my journey through the many stories linked with the lakes and through him I discovered that there were more than 550 lakes in Wales!

After two years of research, I have collected more than 56 different stories and I have included five of these stories in my first book.

Shadows in the Waters seemed to be an appropriate title. I often gazed at the many different waters of the lakes I visited and seemed to see so many shadows, which could have been reflections of the trees and mountains above, but in my fancy, they might just as easily have been the Gwragedd Annwn, wicked Gunnilda, or Gruffudd, the last true Prince of Wales.

I hope that you enjoy reading the stories as much as I have enjoyed writing them.

Margaret Isaac

Acknowledgements

Grateful appreciation is extended to the National History Museum, St. Fagans for permission to print the previously unpublished illustrations relating to Llyn Cwm Llwch, Llyn Safaddon, Kenfig Pool and Llyn-y-Fan Fach. Particular thanks are expressed to Dr. Robin Gwyndaf, Honorary Research Fellow of the National History Museum, for his constant support and encouragement, and to Lowri Jenkins, Archivist, for her assistance with the illustrations.

The illustrations shown in the story of Llyn Llech Owain are included, courtesy of Y Lolfa, having been previously published in full in the book, *King Arthur*, by Gwyn Thomas.

The Mystery of Llyn Cwm Llwch

THE FATHER clasped his daughter's hand. They were kneeling at the side of the beautiful lake of Cwm Llwch. It was Midsummer's Eve and the moon was full.

"Can you see?" whispered the father.

His daughter Catrin screwed up her eyes and peered across the water.

"I think so," she said uncertainly.

"There! There!" her father said excitedly. "She is sitting on the water."

"Look," he said again, "she may disappear and you will never see her again."

Catrin concentrated. It was difficult to see, mists rose above the dark lake and craggy rocks loomed above. Catrin caught her breath. She had suddenly caught sight of a tall beautiful woman, who appeared to be kneeling on the surface of the water. She was perfectly still, gazing into the distance. Her hair flowed over her shoulders to her waist, a gossamer silk gown swept from her shoulders and floated behind her. Catrin could see the woman's reflection in the still water. Even as Catrin gazed at the fairy woman, the form began to melt into the darkness until it could be seen no more.

Father and daughter stood up and stretched themselves. Dafydd had brought his daughter to the lake that Midsummer's Eve. He had promised her that they might be lucky enough to see one of the water fairies known as the Gwragedd Annwn. Dafydd knew a lot about Welsh folklore, although his daughter sometimes thought he was a little fanciful.

Catrin's father was of average height, with dark curly hair and brown eyes. Most people might think he was ordinary looking, but she thought he was the most handsome man she had ever known. Not that she had taken much notice of many other men, apart from her uncles and cousins and the labourers who worked around the farm where they lived.

Catrin was eight years old, growing fast, Dafydd thought, she had a pretty face and fine golden hair tied in two long braids down her back. She had her father's brown eyes.

"Who was she?" she asked.

"She is one of the beautiful Lake Maidens; they are called the Gwragedd Annwn," Dafydd replied.

"Tell me about them again," his daughter said. They sat down on the side of the lake; her father put his arm around his daughter's shoulder and began.

"Long, long ago, in ancient times, people really did live at the bottom of what is now a lake."

His daughter looked puzzled.

"You mean they actually lived underneath the water?"

"No," laughed Dafydd. "Thousands of years ago, where you can now see a lake, the ground was dry, the lake you can see now, Llyn Cwm Llwch, was formed much later," he explained. "People from those times, decided to make their dwelling in this place, because the land was fertile and sheltered. They were a peaceful race, who were gentle, kind people, but they vanished a long time ago. Some say the Gwragedd Annwn, or as they say in English, the Women of the Underworld, are the departed souls of the women who lived in those times."

Dafydd paused and gazed pensively out across the lake.

"Some say, that on Midsummer morning, a door can to be found in a rock by the side of the lake. Long ago, anyone who was brave enough to go through this door, found a secret passage which led them to a small island in the middle of the lake. Here they found a beautiful garden inhabited by the Gwragedd Annwn, who were gracious to their guests and gave them a kind welcome. They offered their human visitors delicious food and entertained them with exquisite music.

Unhappily, on one occasion, one visitor from the land near the lake, angered these beautiful women of the underworld. The Gwragedd Annwn had treated him with their usual warm and gentle hospitality, but he wanted to prove to his friends that he had indeed been entertained by the strange fairy women. So, he stole a flower from their enchanted island. The moment he stepped outside the door in the rock, the flower disappeared and he fell unconscious to the ground! The other guests, had not noticed their friend's theft, and the fairy women showed no outward sign of their displeasure. They politely bade farewell to their visitors who returned safely to their own homes near the lake. But from that day, the door to the magical island has remained firmly shut."

Catrin sighed. "That is a beautiful story," she said, "I wish I could meet those kind women and see their enchanted garden."

"Other people feel the same as you," said her father. "Like us, they come to the side of the lake on Midsummer Eve, hoping to find the door in the rock, but no trace of the fairy island has ever been seen since that time."

Catrin continued to sit thoughtfully by the side of the lake. She played quietly with the dry earth by her side and let some of the fine dust filter through her hand as she imagined what it would have been like, if she could have visited the fairy folk in their enchanted island beneath the lake.

Dafydd continued:

"The local people thought that the Gwragedd Annwn had left the lake, and found a safer place to inhabit. They began to wonder if they might have left behind some treasure. So a group of men decided to drain the lake to see what they could find at the bottom of the lake.

They dug a deep trench in the bank of the lake. Just where they got to the point when another blow with the pick would have broken the bank and let out the water, there was a great flash of lightning and an enormous peal of thunder. The people were terrified and ran back to safety. As they cowered together, they saw a gigantic man rise from the lake.

'You have disturbed the peace of Llyn Cwm Llwch.' The giant's voice was so loud it reverberated around the mountain slopes. 'Take care! I am the Spirit of the Lake, and if you continue, I will make the waters of the lake overflow and flood the valley of the Usk and all of Brecon town.'"

Catrin shuddered. "I'm glad I wasn't there," she said, "I don't think I would have liked the Spirit of the Lake."

Her father put a comforting arm around her shoulder. "I think he was protecting his own territory," he said, "but his warning prevented a disaster too. Brecon and the whole of the valley might have been submerged if the men had continued their digging."

"So what happened next?" asked Catrin.

"The men said that the giant sank back beneath the lake muttering some strange words. They sounded like, 'Remember the cat, remember the cat.'"

"Remember the cat?" said Catrin mystified. "What cat?"

Dafydd continued. "The men were puzzled too. One of them, I think his name was Hywel, said he remembered that when he was younger, he had drowned a cat in Llyn Cwm Llwch. The cat belonged to an old woman and it was very old and sick. It was a black cat with a white star on its forehead. The old lady had tied a little gold bell on a chain around its neck. She was really very fond of her pet but could not bear to see it suffer.

She had asked Hywel to take it away and put it to sleep. This he did.

The next day, he was fishing at Llyn Safaddon, or as they say in English, Llangors Lake. To his great surprise, he saw the cat he had drowned in Llyn Cwm Llwch, floating on the water in the middle of the lake! He recognised its distinctive markings and the gold bell and chain around its neck, but he could not understand how the cat had got there, because the two lakes are about ten miles apart."

"Hywel said that he thought that there must be some kind of underground passage between the two lakes," said Dafydd. "He said that he was sure that if they continued to dig the trench and tried to drain the lake, the waters would overflow and certainly flood Brecon town.

Not only would that happen," he said seriously, "but the water from the smaller lake would flow through the underground passage into the larger lake at Llyn Safaddon, and that would be a disaster, for a large body of water would be discharged over the whole of the Usk valley."

Dafydd paused and looked at his daughter.

"It was lucky the men listened to the Giant and stopped digging the trench then," said Catrin wisely.

"Yes, indeed," replied her father, "otherwise Brecon town would have been flooded and we may not be here today."

Catrin looked thoughtfully at her father, trying to imagine where they would have been if the flood had taken place. She shivered.

"Can we go home now?" she said.

The night air was cold. Catrin stood up and Dafydd wrapped his own large, warm coat around his small daughter.

"Come on then," he said turning away from the lake. "We've had enough story-telling for one day."

They started off down the path leading to their village.

"I like your stories," said Catrin, "are they true?"

"I don't know about that," said Dafydd. "I've been told many stories by many people. I think there is always some truth in them somewhere, and there are many things in life that no-one can explain."

He paused and looked down at the little girl. "Did you enjoy your walk to the lake this evening?"

"Yes," said Catrin soberly. "And we did see that beautiful woman kneeling on the surface of the water of Llyn Cwm Llwch, didn't we?"

"Indeed we did," said her father.

They had reached their front door.

"You won't tell your mother I've been telling you all these tales will you?" said her father.

"I wouldn't dream of it Dad,' laughed Catrin. "She wouldn't believe us would she?"

Dafydd laughed too and hugged his daughter. "I don't suppose she would, but we know better don't we?"

Father and daughter went into their house and closed the door.

Llyn Safaddon: Where No Birds Sing

THE WATERS OF Llyn Safaddon lap gently against green fields where cattle quietly graze. Traces of ancient peoples, farmers, metal smiths, fierce warriors lie buried beneath the cairns and barrows on the brooding hillside. They were content to farm the fertile land, and create wonderful metalwork of gold and bronze, but when their homes were threatened by invaders, then, they defended their land with great bravery and ferocity.

Cadair Arthur, the throne of the great King Arthur, sweeps down majestically from the mountaintops of Pen-y-fan and Corn Du. The ruins of the noble court of Brycheiniog haunt the lake, its splendour savagely destroyed by a cruel Saxon princess. Ranges of hills and mountains protect this pleasant spot from harsher elements, yet the sleepers in the quiet earth exert a brooding presence over the calm water.

People have told many stories about Llyn Safaddon. They say that a monster used to lurk in the water and caused much damage to the lake and to the local people. The monster, known as an afangc, had to be forcibly removed and taken to a higher and more inaccessible place out of harm's way. Others tell of a princess who was so wicked that she and all her people with their whole city were destroyed under an avalanche of water, some say you can still see the tops of these buildings under the water. She was known as Princess Safaddon, the name given to the lake.

Local inhabitants still claim that the lake has many magical properties. Some say that they have seen the water turn bright green, others say it has been known to become scarlet, as if blood were flowing along certain currents and eddies. Some will even tell you that they have seen it covered with buildings or rich pasture lands, or adorned with gardens and orchards. But some people will say anything!

The story you are going to read is one about a real prince, who lived about nine hundred years ago, No-one knows for certain, the year in which he was born but he died in 1137. He was a noble lord, called Gruffudd ap Rhys, brother of the great Princess Nest, husband of the heroic Gwenllian and father of the Lord Rhys.

He lived at the time of Henry I and at the time of this story he was returning from the King's court with Milo and Payn.

* * *

There was once a prince called Gruffudd who was returning to his home in Caeo from the King's court. He was accompanied by two men, Milo or Miles Fitzwalter, Earl of Hereford, Lord of Brecknock, Constable of England, Sheriff of Gloucester, and Payn Fitzjohn, Lord of Ewyas.

It was winter time, and the lake was covered with water fowl of all kinds. Milo noticed that the birds were unusually silent.

"I believe that you are supposed to belong to one of the noblest Welsh families," said Milo. "Of course, all Welshmen claim to have some relationship with their kings and princes, but there are so many, it is hard to know who to believe."

Milo did not like Gruffudd, who had battled long and courageously against the onslaught of the Norman invaders and had been a thorn in King Henry's side for many years.

"I am a true descendant of the princes of Wales," replied Gruffudd, "I have no wish to quarrel with you, but perhaps I have more right to these lands than you two gentlemen."

Milo reddened, for he knew that Henry had grudgingly bestowed the lordship of Caeo on Gruffudd in an attempt to placate him. Milo liked to think of his own high titles, Earl of Hereford, Lord of Brecknock, Constable of England, Sheriff of Gloucester; they had a certain ring about them, he thought.

"You see that the birds gathered before us on the lake, are silent," Gruffudd continued. "It is an ancient saying in Wales," his voice held a challenge, "that if the true born Prince of the country passing near Llyn Safaddon, should order the birds to sing they will immediately obey."

Gruffudd, although no longer rich, retained a dignified and noble bearing. He understood the nature and vanity of the other man.

"Since you are now Lord and Master of this land of Brecknock, then you should give the command."

Milo could not but agree to this suggestion. Feeling very foolish, he addressed the birds:

"Water creatures of Llyn Safaddon, I, Miles Fitzwalter, Earl of Hereford, Lord of Brecknock, Constable of England, Sheriff of Gloucester, he paused, command you to burst forth into song before your lawful master."

The birds stirred, some flapped their wings, some glided across the water, some preened their feathers; all were silent.

Much discomfited, Milo said, "I think I have proved that these Welsh tales are really nonsensical fantasy, fit only for children."

"Perhaps, before we make up our minds on that point," said Gruffudd, "Payn Fitzjohn, should make an attempt, for he has some stake in the ownership of the land. He was born in Ewyas, and is now lord of that region. Perhaps the birds will sing for him."

Payn Fitzjohn, a friend of Milo's, hoped to make some further advancement in his fortunes from his acquaintance with the greater man. However, he was also aware that he was indeed born a Welshman, unlike Milo.

He stood at the lakeside and drew himself up to his full height (for he was rather short in stature).

"I bid the feathered folk of the lake, I mean the birds who should cheer us with melodious singing, to enchant their true prince, Payn Fitzjohn Lord of Ewyas, with the music of the heavens."

He looked at Gruffudd and Milo triumphantly, proud of his poetic language.

The birds however, again did not respond in voice, but all seemed to fall asleep.

"I think you may have fatigued them with your high sounding phrases," said Gruffudd, "they show no inclination to make even the smallest sound."

Gruffudd stood at the side of the lake and looked at the birds sitting silent on the water. He went down on one knee and cried out, "Dear Lord, you know all things, if you have created me the true Prince of Wales, I will be bold and bid these birds to break their silence, so that their song will show the beauty of your creation!" Gruffudd stood up and raised his hands towards the birds, immediately they began beating the water with their wings, and flew upwards to the skies, singing in unison with their beautiful bird-song."

The people of their party gathered on the shore of the lake were astonished at the sight. "Surely, this is a sign from God that Gruffudd is indeed the true Prince of Wales, the rightful owner of the land now claimed by Milo Fitzwalter and Payn Fitzjohn, with the authority of King Henry."

Disconcerted and dismayed Milo and Payn Fitzjohn hastily returned to court and related all that had happened at Safaddon to the King.

Lake Stories of Wales

After some consideration, Henry replied with an oath:

"I am not surprised. We have assumed authority over the land, by violence and wrongdoing, but it is well known by the people and others that Gruffudd and his relatives are the true inheritors of the land of Wales."

Although he said this privately to Milo and Payn Fitzjohn, he did not publicise his words, neither did the strange happening of the birdsong at Safaddon change his ways for he continued to exert his rule over the country for many years to come.

Kenfig Pool:
The Curse of the Pantannas

MANY YEARS AGO, the stretch of water now known as Kenfig Pool, did not exist. Instead the land was inhabited by people seeking a pleasant, fertile place in which to build their homes. The small community were happy for many hundreds of years, and, at the time of this story, they lived by rules which ensured a peaceful, well organised society; some were butchers and bakers, some looked after horses and were called ostlers, some, the politicians of the day, were aldermen and burgesses. Most people had their own smallholdings, where they kept pigs and chickens, and occasionally, one or two cows. They enjoyed a simple way of life, working hard during the week and attending church on Sundays. Like most people, some were bad and some were good, but the aldermen and burgesses and the church elders kept the peace with strict laws.

The land of Kenfig was owned by Gilbert de Clare, Earl of Gloucester and Hereford. He had a daughter, Gunnilda, whom he idolised. She was beautiful and she was spoilt and she grew up to be selfish and greedy. Her wickedness caused the greatest tragedy known to Kenfig. This is the story of how her villainy destroyed the town and flooded the land. It is the story of the birth of Kenfig Pool.

* * *

Many men had fallen in love with Gunnilda and, at the time of our story, she realised it was time to seek a husband. One particular lover caught her fancy, he was handsome and he adored her, but unfortunately, he was poor and Gunnilda wanted a man of great wealth.

"I would marry you," she said, "but you have no money and I must have a husband who is rich.

I cannot live without good things around me, so I am afraid that unless you can bring me gold enough to satisfy me, I must seek another husband. I do not care how you do it, I am not one who looks too closely at the manner in which I can enjoy myself, rules and laws mean nothing to me, unless they help me to live as I please." Although she was so beautiful she really was a very selfish and cruel woman

Madoc, her lover, was besotted and could not bear the thought of anyone else marrying this beautiful lady. So he determined to find a way to acquire enough gold to satisfy Gunnilda, by any means within his power.

Griffith was one of the village elders. He was rich, but he was wise. He was a skilled musician and poet and the people loved to listen to his stories on cold winter evenings when they gathered together in the village hall. Madoc knew Griffith well, and decided to find a way to rob the old man of his gold.

It was a dark night in December. Griffith had been telling his stories to the village people in the hall, and they had ended a happy evening's entertainment singing songs and telling old tales, before braving the cold night air to hurry to their homes. Griffith's home lay on the outskirts of the village. His path lay along a quiet isolated lane, with hedgerows either side. The bushes bore no leaves and the skeletal branches of the trees hardly moved in the cold night air.

As Griffith walked briskly towards a bend in the road, he thought he heard a movement, and looked behind him. He fancied he had heard a footstep, and he felt a little shiver run down his spine. He quickened his step. A figure loomed out of the dark and Griffith felt a sharp sickening blow to his head. His body fell to the ground in a heap. Griffith lay still. He was dead. Madoc moved nearer to the body and bent over to examine it. Satisfied that he had indeed murdered his victim, Madoc walked swiftly to Griffith's house. He broke open the door and entered.

Madoc knew Griffith's house well, he had often been invited with other neighbours to chat and talk over past times. So he knew where Griffith kept his gold. Madoc went to the little room which

Griffith kept for his small community gatherings. In the corner was a wooden chest. Madoc broke open the clasp and lifted the lid. He put his hand inside and lifted out a large sack. It was full of gold. He slung it over his shoulder and turned towards the door. As he did so, there was a great sigh, which seemed to come from someone within the room. Madoc stopped and peered into the darkness but the room was empty. He moved nearer to the door and again he heard a deep sigh. This time he moved swiftly out of the room and out of the house. But, as he walked quickly down the lane towards his own home with the sack on his shoulder, the sighing became louder, and Madoc heard a ghostly voice behind him. At first he could not hear the words, but the voice grew louder until he could hear the words distinctly.

"Vengeance is coming; Vengeance is coming." Madoc did not look back, he ran all the way to his own home, where he entered and shut and bolted his door. Breathing heavily, he threw the sack of gold into the corner of his bedroom and climbed into bed. He pulled the clothes over his ears, he was shaking with fright. Gradually, sleep overcame him and when he awoke he saw the weak rays of a winter sun shining through his bedroom window.

Things looked a lot better to Madoc in the fresh morning light. He thought of his beautiful lady, Gunnilda, and of her delight when she would see his new found wealth. He quickly forgot the evil murder and the threatening voices in his eagerness to embrace his new life.

Of course, Gunnilda was now very happy to marry Madoc. He told her how he had acquired his wealth but she did not care. She was happy to have married a handsome suitor with plenty of gold, how he had obtained it, did not trouble her at all.

The villagers were devastated when they discovered the body of Griffith lying in the road the following morning. They buried him sorrowfully and mourned him greatly, but they could not discover his murderer

Madoc and Gunnilda invited many guests to their wedding. It was a splendid celebration and lasted three days and three nights. Gunnilda invited all the important people from the neighbourhood, but there were not many of the local people at the wedding. After all they could not afford to bring Gunnilda rich presents.

The villagers did not want to be invited, they thought that their lady was far too proud and haughty, and she had been very cruel to them in many ways.

Months later, Gunnilda overheard her servants whispering together, they stopped as she approached.

"What were you saying, that you could not let me hear?" she demanded angrily.

"We have heard some gossip," replied one of the bolder servants, "that Griffith's grave is haunted and that his spirit will not rest while his murderer goes free."

Gunnilda was disquieted by the servant's words and went to Madoc and told him what she had heard.

"You must go to Griffith's grave and try to lay this ghost," she said.

Reluctantly, Madoc did as he was bid, for he dared not disobey his headstrong wife and one dark night, he set out for Griffith's grave.

Griffith was buried in the quiet churchyard. Yew trees guarded the entrance to the church where the dead souls rested in the quiet earth. On the night that Madoc chose to visit the grave of his murdered victim, the sky was dark and the wind moaned through the trees. Madoc crept as close as he dared to the side of the grave. He shivered. He knew that he had to try to lay the ghost the servants had gossiped about; the ghost that Gunnilda wanted him to silence. But he did not feel very brave or confident, in fact he felt decidedly frightened. He was the murderer and Griffith, his victim, was now a spirit, beyond his power.

Madoc stood still and listened. He looked up at the dark sky through the branches of the trees. He saw the moon, a crescent moon moving slowly through the sky. There was no sound except that of the breeze rustling through the trees. Then he heard a strange whispering, it sounded like a scrabbling and scratching and at first he thought it might be a night creature snuffling in the long grasses in a marshy patch of ground near the grave. The whispering became louder and he suddenly heard an eerie voice, such as the one he had heard on the night he killed Griffith:

"Is not this innocent man to be avenged?"

Madoc quaking in his shoes, looked around to see if he could see the person who spoke. He could see nothing but the trees, the sky, the moon and the stars. He looked at Griffith's grave. A few scattered leaves around the grave fluttered.

"Vengeance will come," said a second voice. "This innocent soul will be avenged. *Hyd y nawfed âch*, a terrible fate will befall the evildoers and the innocent will be avenged."

The voices died away. Madoc opened his eyes. He had closed them in fear as he listened to the ghostly words. He looked around him again. His body was shaking, he felt giddy, but in the sacred place nothing stirred.

Madoc stood up, he turned to make his way home, but he found that his feet seemed to be fixed to the ground. He looked up and saw the moon emerging from behind the trees.

"Everything is as it should be," he thought, "the moon is in the sky, the yew trees have not moved, the church is still standing," he looked down at his own body. "I am still in one piece." He straightened his shoulders. "I must be resolute, and return to my dearest wife to recount to her all that has happened, she will know what to do." He shook himself and began walking in the direction of his home. But as he heard the wind rustling through the trees, he quickened his pace and soon left the graveyard.

Madoc sought out his wife in the early hours of the following morning and recounted his adventures of the previous night. He told her of the voices.

"I heard one voice whispering, 'Is not this innocent man to be avenged?' he said. And then another replying, 'this innocent soul will be avenged *hyd y nawfed âch*, then a terrible fate will befall the evildoers and the innocent will be avenged.'"

Madoc shivered as he remembered, but Gunnilda looked puzzled.

"I don't understand the strange words from another tongue, what were they?"

Madoc replied, *"hyd y nawfed âch."* They are words in the language of the Welsh, moreover, they are the ancient words of the Pantannas. I fear that this is the curse of the Pantannas." He shuddered again.

"Explain what this means." Gunnilda was not familiar with the Welsh language or the old Welsh ways, and she spoke impatiently.

Madoc replied in a low voice, "The Pantannas are an ancient people long dead, whose spirits still haunt the earth. They become restless when they feel that someone has disrupted the old way of life and they wreak their own revenge on the perpetrators. Griffith was a wise man and kept the old tales alive with his music and his old tales. The Pantannas would not be happy at his death."

Gunnilda asked again, "Tell me the meaning of the strange words."

"*Hyd y nawfed âch* means 'up to the ninth degree'," replied Madoc. "It means that the Pantannas intend to wreak vengeance on us, the evildoers, within the ninth generation."

"Does that mean that this terrible thing, whatever it may be, is to happen in the time of the ninth generation of our descendants?" she asked.

"I suppose so," said Madoc. He hesitated, "I don't trust fairy language, it is never what it seems to be."

"I am not so foolish," said Gunnilda briskly. "We will be long dead, beneath the mould, I think, if this fate is to befall our descendants within the ninth generation. That is, if all this happened anyway, the whole thing may be nothing but your feverish imagination."

Madoc still looked frightened and anxious, he remembered the voices after his killing of Griffith and his visit to the graveyard. He was not as confident as his wife that it was all fancy. But she was the stronger one.

She said briskly, "So, we have nothing to fear, nothing will happen to us." Her face brightened.

"Come my brave lover," she said, cheerfully, "let's forget the voices and the ghosts and the body of Griffith lying in his cold grave. We have gold enough to spend however we wish. Let us enjoy life and live for the day. If vengeance is to come, it will not come in our time!"

And so they ignored the voices and the strange words of the Pantannas. The lady and her lover felt safe enough and lived an unrestrained riotous existence. They spared themselves nothing in the way of indulgence or wealth. They grasped anything which gave them pleasure with no thought for the suffering it might cause others. They had many children and grandchildren and great grand children who were as wicked as Madoc and Gunnilda. They had no thought for the townsfolk, who became very poor and very miserable. Many left Kenfig, until the only ones remaining were the relatives and descendants of Madoc and Gunnilda.

And so Gunnilda and her lover lived for many years with their children and children's children who were equally selfish, thinking only of making money to spend on their own pleasures and gaining their wealth by any means possible, through murder and theft.

One day, they decided to hold a magnificent feast in their castle, to celebrate their marriage, their wealth and their success. Gunnilda and Madoc invited every member of their family to this feast, all their children and all their children's children, their cousins and aunts and uncles, everyone who was related to the great Lady Gunnilda and her husband Madoc.

Gunnilda had heard of a man who lived in a remote village not far from Kenfig. He was renowned for his skill in telling tales and making music on his harp. She invited him to attend the great banquet to entertain her guests. Somewhat surprisingly, he agreed, for most people who lived outside the town of Kenfig were reluctant to spend any time in that place.

The party was at its height, and the revellers were enjoying the food and entertainment, when a voice was heard from outside the castle. The revellers gathered near the window and looked out. They saw the harpist standing on the ramparts of the castle, in his hand a great burning torch.

"I am Griffith, the *goresgynnydd*, the descendant of the man murdered by Madoc, *o fewn y nawfed âch*," he shouted. "Vengeance has come, even to the ninth generation!" With these words he hurled the torch into the castle. The curtains and timber immediately caught alight and soon the castle was blazing. Waters rushed down from the moat and the river and flooded the town of Kenfig, until the land was covered with water and nothing remained but the lake which can be seen to this day.

Griffith leapt to safety and ran toward the water. As he looked across the lake from the shore, he saw some small, dark, sodden objects floating towards him. He bent down to pick them up. Turning them over in his hand he saw that they were two black gloves.

He smiled as he saw the name Griffith that was inscribed on each of the gloves. "*Griffith*," he said to himself, "my namesake, murdered so many years ago by Madoc to serve the evil desire of his lady Gunnilda. So the words of the Pantannas have been fulfilled, I am the goresgynnydd, the grandson born to the ninth degree *o fewn y nawfed âch*. Now Griffith, my ancestor, your spirit can rest in peace."

The castle lay in silent ruins. The waters of Kenfig Pool rippled in the moonlight. The harpist turned and walked away from the ruined castle and the buried town of Kenfig and made his way slowly home towards Margam and the Abbey.

Llyn Llech Owain:
Arthur's Greatest Knight

ARTHUR WAS IN his castle at Caerleon on Usk, celebrating Whitsuntide. He sat in the centre of the great chamber on a seat of rushes over which was spread a covering of red silk with a cushion of red silk beneath his elbow. With him were Owain, son of Urien, Kynon son of Clydno and Cai son of Cyner with many other knights. Gwenhwyfar, Arthur's wife, sat by the window, sewing and chatting with her guests. Arthur felt very happy. Owain had returned to Caerleon after three long years' absence, and Arthur had missed him.

"Well, Owain," said Arthur, "I am glad to have you with me once more, but I and the rest of this company know little of your adventures while you have been away. I am sure that you have much to tell us and we are very ready to listen."

Owain smiled.

"I, too, am glad to be here to enjoy your company and that of all my friends. You may recall a similar occasion before I went away when we sat in this same place and listened to Kynon describing an adventure he had experienced. I was deeply affected by his story and vowed to see for myself the strange places and people that Kynon had encountered.

So I set off and travelled the length and breadth of my own country and throughout far distant regions, until one day, I chanced upon the fairest valley I had ever seen in the world, where every tree was in its perfect beauty. A river ran through the valley and a path ran alongside the river. I followed the path until mid-day and continued on my journey through the valley until the evening when I came to the end of a great expanse of level ground. There I saw a large shining castle at the foot of which was a rushing stream of water.

As I approached the castle, a little way off, I saw a handsome looking man, dressed in clothes made of golden silk, and his shoes fastened with golden buckles.

'Good day sir,' I said walking towards him.

'Good morning to you, Sir Knight,' he said courteously.

'As you can see,' I continued, 'I am a stranger in these parts. I have come a long way and I am hungry and thirsty.' I rubbed my chin ruefully. 'I am also in need of a good shave and a bath.'

'We welcome strangers,' he replied. 'Come with me and I will see what I can do to help you.'

He then led me towards the castle where the porter at the gate allowed us both to enter. When we entered the great hall, I saw twenty-four maidens sitting by a window embroidering on fine silk cloth. I have never seen any maiden so beautiful as these, except, of course, the Lady Gwenhwyfar who is indeed the loveliest of women." Gwenhwyfar looked up from her seat in the window and bowed her head towards Owain with a graceful smile.

Owain continued.

"The maidens looked after my horses and invited me to bathe and put on fresh clothes. Afterwards they led me to a table where they had prepared a splendid meal. I sat at the table with my host and I ate heartily, for I was very hungry and the food and wine were excellent. While we were eating, the man asked me for my name.

I replied, 'My name is Owain ap Urien.'

'I am pleased to receive you here Owain,' said he, 'may I ask what brings you to this castle?'

'I am a knight of King Arthur's Court; I have come to seek an adventure and to challenge myself against someone worthy of combat, to see if I can gain mastery over him.'

The man looked at me and smiled.

'I have heard much of King Arthur's knights, their courage and reputation, but I think I can direct you to a combat with a worthy opponent. Sleep here tonight and, in the morning, rise early and take the road upwards through the valley until you reach a wood. Soon, you will come to a road branching off to the right; follow this road until you come to a sheltered glade with a large mound in the centre. You will see a giant standing on top of the mound. He has but one foot and one eye in the middle of his forehead. He holds a fearsome club made of iron. He is very ill-favoured to look on and he is the Keeper of that wood. You will see a thousand wild animals grazing around him. Ask him the way out of the glade. Do not be put off by his discourteous manner, for he will point out the directions you seek.'

I went to bed, but sleep did not come easily, for I tossed and turned all night, thinking of the things that had happened to me, and wondering what the morrow might bring. The next morning, I rose and dressed, equipping myself for the adventure which was promised me. I mounted my horse and started on my journey following the directions given to me by my host. I rode through the valley to the wood, and followed the road until I arrived at the glade.

I was astonished at the number of wild animals I saw grazing round about the mound in the centre of the glade. Then I caught sight of the giant standing on the top of the mound as the man had said he would be. He surely was a huge creature and his iron club was indeed a fearsome sight, I am sure that it would have been too heavy for four ordinary men to lift.

He fixed me with his one eye, but I spoke out boldly.

'Could you tell me the way out of the glade?'

He responded curtly. 'Take that road,' he said, pointing with his great iron club.

I hesitated, overcome with curiosity, and gestured to the many wild animals grazing around him.

'What control do you have over all these creatures?' I said.

'I will show you, little man,' he said contemptuously.

He took his club in his hand and he struck a stag a great blow with his club so that it brayed vehemently. At the sound of the stag, all the animals came together and they were as numerous as the stars in the sky. Indeed, I had little room to stand in the glade among them. And amongst the many different kinds of animals I saw serpents and dragons. The giant fixed them with his eye and bade them go and feed, and they bowed their heads and meekly did as he had bid them, as a vassal would to a lord.

The giant looked at me triumphantly. 'Now, you see what authority I have over these creatures,' he said boastfully.

'Indeed I do,' I replied meekly, 'and I am sure that such a powerful man will find it easy to give me the assistance I seek and show me the way out of this glade.'

'Take the path which leads towards the top of the glade,' he replied, mollified by my courteous tone, 'and climb the wooded slope until you come to the summit. There you will find an open space like a large valley and in the middle of the glade you will see a tall tree whose branches are greener that the greenest pine tree. Under this tree is a fountain and by the side of the fountain is a marble slab and on the marble slab a silver bowl attached to the slab by a silver chain so that it cannot be taken away.'

The big man paused.

'Take the bowl and throw a bowlful of water upon the slab and you will hear a mighty peal of thunder so loud that you will think that heaven and earth are trembling with fury. With the thunder will come a heavy shower of hailstones so severe that you will think you will not be able to endure it. After the shower of hailstones, the weather will become fair, but every leaf that was upon the tree will have been carried away by the shower. Then a flight of birds will come and alight upon the tree and sing more sweetly than you have ever heard anywhere in your own country. As you become enchanted with the birdsong, you will hear a noise of murmuring and complaining coming towards you along the valley.'

The Giant seemed amused as he continued.

'You will see a knight upon a coal-black horse clothed in black velvet, and with a pennon of black linen upon his lance. He will ride towards you at great speed to challenge you. If you flee from him he will overtake you and if you stay he will surely unseat you and fling you from your horse. If you do not find trouble from this adventure you will never find it again for the rest of your life.'

I was amazed and waited eagerly for the giant to continue, but the huge man fell silent and seemed to take no further interest in my presence. So I left him standing there on top of the mound surrounded by his kingdom of wild animals, and I journeyed on, until I reached the top of the wooded slope and there I found everything as the giant had described to me. I went up to the tree and beneath it I saw the fountain, and by its side a marble slab, the silver bowl on the ground, fastened by a silver chain. I took the bowl and I threw a bowlful of water upon the slab and immediately there came a mighty clap of thunder even more violent than the giant had led me to expect. After the thunder, came the shower of hailstones and, I tell you my friends, I was scarcely able to endure the force of the shower. Each of the hailstones seemed to stab through my skin and flesh until it reached the bone.

I turned my horse's shank towards the shower and placed the front of my shield over his head and neck, while I held the upper part of it over my own head. Only in this way could I withstand the force of the shower. Then the sky cleared and when I looked on the tree there was not a single leaf left upon it. The birds alighted on the tree and sang. I have never heard so sweet a sound. And as I listened to this enchanting sound, I heard a murmuring and complaining along the valley and a voice crying aloud,

'What has brought you to this place, Sir Knight? What harm have my people done to you that you should act in this way towards our land? Did you know what you were doing? When you seized the silver bowl and cast the water on to the marble slab, you created the dreadful and unnatural storm of hailstones, which exposed all who live in my kingdom to their dreadful force. Everything has been destroyed because of your actions. I am the Keeper of the Fountain and Guardian of this dominion. It is my duty now to challenge you to mortal combat?'

As I heard these words, so a knight on a black horse appeared, clothed in jet black velvet with a pennon of black linen that covered his lance. We immediately charged each other, and fought fiercely. The fighting was so violent, that we broke each other's lances, quickly drew our swords and continued fighting relentlessly, with no quarter given or taken. Finally, I struck a mighty blow to the knight's head and cut his helmet in two, cleaving through almost to the brain. Mortally wounded, the Black Knight managed to turn his horse's head and flee back to the castle, and I followed in close pursuit.

The Black Knight reached the portcullis of his castle, and the porter recognising his lord, quickly raised the gate to let him through. However, to prevent my entry into the castle, he lowered the gate with such speed and force that the portcullis hurtled downwards and cut my poor horse in two, so that the rear part was outside the castle while I remained between the gates astride the front part!

I would have remained in this terrible predicament, in sore need of assistance if I had not discovered a true friend. She was a beautiful maiden called Luned.

In spite of my uncomfortable position astride the front half of my horse, I must have dozed, for I woke in the early hours of the dawn the next day. I heard a woman's voice above me.

'Good heavens,' she cried.

I looked up to see a pretty face staring down at me.

'As you can see,' I said, feeling somewhat discomfited, 'I am in no state to open the gate,' and, I added, a little discourteously, 'I don't see how a young girl like you will be able to help me either.' I must admit I felt foolish and undignified in front of that steady gaze.

The girl smiled to herself, as if she knew more than she was willing to tell.

'Before I offer to help you, you must tell me your name.'

'I am called Owain ap Urien,' I said, 'and I am a knight of King Arthur.'

'Well, Owain ap Urien, let me see if I can help you out of your predicament,' she said, and leaning over the wall, she pulled a ring from her finger and held it out to me. I stretched out my hand and just managed to take hold of the ring.

'Keep the ring safely in the palm of your hand, so that no-one is able to see the stone in the centre,' she said. 'As long as the stone is hidden from sight, no-one will be able to see the person who holds the ring.'

I looked curiously at the band of gold resting in the palm of my hand. Set in its centre was a large blue sparkling sapphire.

'The knights in the castle are looking for you. They will certainly put you to death if they find you, but you will be safe as long as you hide the stone, for that will make you invisible. Soon they will come to the castle walls, to seek you in the countryside beyond the castle. When they open the castle gates, you will be able to slip inside. I will be waiting for you, near that horseblock.' She pointed in the direction of the horseblock near the gate. 'I will not be able to see you either, but if you put your hand on my shoulder, I will lead you to a safe place. My name is Luned and I serve the Lady who owns the castle.'

I would have liked to question this mysterious young girl further, but as soon as she had finished speaking, she disappeared from view. I thought she might be leading me into yet more trouble, but trapped as I was between the two castle gates, with my horse cut in two and the other half of the poor creature outside the castle walls, I seemed to have no alternative but to follow her instructions. At least, if she was able to free me, I would be in a better position to confront any further dangers.

So I hid the ring in my hand and waited. I heard the knights marching around on the other side of the castle walls, probably looking for me as Luned had predicted. I heard the gates being opened, and soldiers appeared, looking everywhere for me. I quickly dismounted and slipped past the men to make my way to where Luned was waiting near the horseblock, as she had promised. She gave a little shudder as she felt my invisible hand on her shoulder, but she gave no further sign and led me inside the castle to a large and beautiful room.

She looked around her; I was still clutching the ring tightly and remained invisible. I opened the palm of my hand and exposed the blue sapphire.

'Ah!' she cried, as she saw me standing before her, 'I am glad to see you followed my instructions. You are safe from harm for the time being. You can bathe and change here,' she continued. 'I have prepared some hot water and some fresh clothes for you.'

After I had bathed and changed, I felt refreshed. Luned had prepared a meal for me and I had never tasted such magnificent food, or drank such delicious wine; I was very hungry and I ate and drank heartily. Then overcome with tiredness I slept soundly until late the next day.

I was awakened by a clamour of bells and great groaning. Startled, I jumped up. Luned was sitting quietly on a couch near me.

'What is that noise,' I cried.

'The knight who owns the castle is dying,' she said.

I fell silent.

Not long afterwards, an even greater noise came from outside my window.

I looked outside and saw a solemn procession of men, boys, and weeping women. They were all dressed in black and followed a coffin borne on a magnificent hearse drawn by four jet black horses. The women were led by the most beautiful lady I had ever seen.

'What has happened now,' I cried, greatly agitated.

'The knight is dead. He was my Lady's husband,' said Luned quietly. 'She is now quite helpless and quite alone. He was a noble and courageous man who guarded the Fountain and all the land from danger. Now that he is dead, these lands may be lost and the Fountain will be in grave danger.'

'What kind of danger?' I asked. 'Why is it so important to guard the Fountain?'

'The Fountain is as old as time,' said Luned, 'and should it fall prey to savages or wild animals, a deluge would cover the land and perhaps time itself would cease. My mistress is the Lady of the Fountain. It is in her keeping, and she must see that it is always protected. To do this, she needs a champion who will promise to be her Keeper of the Fountain.'

'Then it is my duty to take the place of the lady's husband,' I cried chivalrously. 'I am to blame for her dilemma, for I caused his death and it is for me to make amends.'

'My Lady certainly needs a champion now that her husband is dead. You proved that you were the stronger man when you struck the Black Knight with a mortal blow. Perhaps you are most fitting to take his place.'

'I do not think she is likely to agree with you,' muttered Owain, 'she won't accept her husband's murderer.'

'Then I must try to persuade her,' said Luned. 'You must make yourself look a fitting champion and present yourself to her.' Luned rose from the couch. 'In the meantime, I will go and speak to her.'

Everything happened just as Luned promised."

Owain was coming to the end of his tale. His companions had listened to his story with great interest.

"She persuaded her mistress that she needed a fitting champion to look after her lands and the ancient Fountain on which so much depended. She praised my courage and suggested that a knight of king Arthur would be the best choice in place of the devoted and brave husband she had lost. Although the lady was at first reluctant to accept the man who had defeated her lord, she realised that Luned's advice was the best and wisest course.

She agreed to meet me, and I presented myself to her with all the courtesy and demeanour of one of Arthur's knights. She looked on me with favour and accepted me as the Keeper of the Fountain and I fought fiercely to protect it from many savages and wild creatures. This I did for three years. Then, as you know, my lord King, you arrived with Kai and others and persuaded my lady to let me return with you for a short time. And here I am, ready to serve you as you wish.

That is the end of my story," he said.

Arthur and the company fell silent for a while, thinking of all the amazing adventures that Owain had described. Then Arthur said, "I have heard many tales of the adventures of my knights, but your adventures Owain are the most marvellous I have heard."

The rest of the knights agreed with their king, and they all celebrated Owain's return to Arthur's court for many days and nights.

Sadly, Owain neglected his promise to return to the Lady and the castle and he became engaged in many other fierce and exciting adventures. He did return many years later and gave her assistance in defeating her enemies, but he never again remained with her at the castle to take on the defence of her lands and become the Keeper of the Fountain.

* * *

Many years later, Owain was riding alone through the valley near the fountain. He was wet through to his skin. His great bay horse trotted forward, stumbling occasionally. It looked tired and forlorn, its wet mane stuck lankly to its neck, as it pushed forward in response to the touch of the reins in its master's hand. He had ridden through a savage thunderstorm, with heavy hailstones following the rain. Now the sun had come out and Owain looked around him for a place to rest. He recognised familiar slopes surrounding the familiar spring and decided to make his way there to rest and drink before continuing his journey. He dismounted and used his great strength to lift the stone away from the spring and allow his faithful horse to drink. Then he too drank long and deep. He lay on the ground resting, until the warmth of the sun made him drowsy, and, overcome by tiredness, he fell asleep.

Unfortunately, he was so overcome with fatigue that he forgot to replace the large stone which covered the spring.

While he slept in the heather, Owain dreamed of raging torrents of water surrounding him. He felt as if he was falling into deep water and drowning, the dream was so real. He awoke with a start to find that water was indeed lapping around his ankles.

He leapt to his feet and saw a great lake in front of him. He looked for the spring, but could not see it! Too late, he realised that he had forgotten to replace the stone! The spring had disappeared! All he could see was a large lake of water growing ever larger and deeper and threatening to submerge him and his horse and all the land surrounding him.

Owain was frantic. He knew that he would have to do something quickly to stop the water from submerging the land. Some strange instinct seemed to guide him and he leapt onto his horse and rode to higher ground. Horse and rider galloped around the lake, once, twice, three times.

Each time, the force of the water seemed to subside, stopping the welling water from flooding the surrounding land, until at last Owain drew his horse to a standstill. He looked out over a great water. The blue-grey lake glistened calm and full. Owain looked in vain for a sign of the great stone and the magic spring, but it seemed as if they had never been.

Yet, as Owain gazed out into the centre of the lake he noticed the ripple of the water, and a few bubbles rose to the surface and then disappeared. Owain thought of the spring which would never be seen again, he imagined what would have happened if he had not acted quickly to prevent the water from flooding the land.

Owain was so ashamed at what he had done that he returned to his cave at Craig y Ddinas in Llandybie and was never seen again. It is said that he and his knights sleep there and will only awake at the hour of their country's direst need.

The lake is now known as Llyn Llech Owain, or as it is known in English, The Lake of Owain's Stone.

The Lady of Llyn-y-Fan Fach

To visit Llyn-y-Fan, you will have to know the way, for it is well hidden from the common tourist.

It lies seven miles to the South of Llandovery near the village of Myddfai. You will pass quiet farms, forest plantations, and pretty hedgerows, full of wild flowers. As you come to a crossroads, you will find an inn and a signpost to Llyn-y-Fan Fach. Here, the road becomes rougher until it becomes a mere track. A youth hostel stands on the right and a little further on, a church stands on a corner. As you continue, you will pass clean-looking farm buildings, and horses grazing. Eventually, you cross a cattle grid, and begin to climb upwards along a rough track. Smooth boulders tumble down the hillside, weathered over many years into different shapes and sizes, with white quartz stones lying on the ground. Water tumbles over rocks and stones and sheep perch precariously on vertical inclines or jump sure-footed across streams. The strange silence is broken only by the babbling of the water and the sound of distant voices.

To reach the lake, you walk across clumpy, mountain grass to the water's edge. Bluey-grey Pennant Sandstone escarpments drop down to the lake. In springtime, bluebells, dandelions, white cuckoo kings, yellow celandines and cow parsley scatter along the hedgerows; violets grow on grassy banks, and there are rock pools.

The lake is protected on two sides by mountains which rise to many metres. There are flat grasslands on the other sides leading to shallow water. Here Nelfach walked from the lake leading her cattle as a dowry to the waiting Rhiwallon.

The sky is blue, the clouds like swans' feathers. There are no people, only the sound of the water, and the breeze blowing against your face.

A raven sits on a pole.

More than eight hundred years ago, at the close of the Twelfth Century, a widow lived on a small farm in a village called Blaensawdde, two miles distant from the lake. Her husband had been killed in the fighting against the Princes of South Wales, and she was left alone to bring up her only son. Despite her difficulties, she had increased her livestock to such an extent that she did not have sufficient pastureland near her home and had sent a portion of her cattle to graze on the adjoining Black Mountain. A favourite place for grazing lay near the small lake of Llyn-y-Fan Fach.

The widow had a son called Rhiwallon. When he had grown to manhood, he inherited the farm from his mother, who had become too frail to manage the farm alone.

One day, Rhiwallon was sitting on a small grassy hillock by the side of the lake, idly contemplating a beautiful brown calf lying by the side of a large brown and white cow, who was chewing the cud by the side of the still water.

His gaze moved to the middle of the lake, where he was startled by a vision of a beautiful maiden sitting on the surface of the water, combing her hair with a golden comb. Her graceful form appeared to be as translucent as gossamer, her skin as snow-white as the foam of the lake, her eyes as emerald-green as the water and her hair was like the gold of the sun.

Suddenly the lissom figure shifted and changed, transforming itself into two images, one rising above the water; one reflected beneath its glassy surface. Rhiwallon was transfixed. He stood up and shook himself, he thought he must be dreaming.

He had some bread in his hand, and, not knowing why, he held out his hand and offered her the bread. She glided closer towards him, and he attempted to touch her, but she gently eluded him and disappeared into the lake. Rhiwallon, entranced with her beauty, was disappointed and wished that he had been able to make some further acquaintance with the strange maiden.

When he returned home, he told his mother of this amazing vision.

"I offered her some bread," he explained, "but she refused and disappeared back into the water."

His mother considered her son gravely:

"The bread was over-baked, such a dainty creature would be unable to accept it. I will bake you another loaf, and we shall see if you will be able to win her with a second attempt."

So, his mother baked another loaf for Rhiwallon and he returned to the lake a second time. He sat by the side of the lake for many hours, in vain, for he saw no sign of the maiden. Then he noticed his cattle making their way to the mountainous side of the lake, although the grass was not so good there. Puzzled, Rhiwallon followed them and saw beneath the slope of the mountain, seated on the water, the beautiful maiden, combing her long golden hair as he had seen her before.

Rhiwallon offered her the second piece of bread that his mother had baked for him. Again the maiden shook her head, but she smiled as she disappeared beneath the water.

The memory of her encouraging smile, gave Rhiwallon a little hope. He returned home and recounted to his mother his second meeting.

"She did not accept my offer of bread," he said, "but she smiled at me before she disappeared once more into the water."

"I must have baked the bread too soft this time," she said, "we must try a loaf which is neither too hard nor too soft."

So his mother baked some bread for the third time and gave it to her son. Rhiwallon drove his cattle to the lake once more, with the moderately-baked bread in his pocket. He waited by the lake all day long until the sun was setting. Finally, with a deep sigh, he made ready to depart, thinking that the maiden would appear no more. He began to collect the cattle and turned with a heavy heart for home, taking one last look over his shoulder. To his surprise, he saw several cattle walking on the surface of the water!

He watched anxiously, hoping that this unusual sight meant that he would soon see his mysterious lady, once more. He was not disappointed, for soon, she too re-appeared behind the cattle, walking on the surface of the water! As she approached the shore, he ran to meet her and she smiled as he reached for her hand, nor did she refuse the bread he offered her.

"I think that time does not mean the same to you in the world where you live, as it does to me," said Rhiwallon, "I have waited long to see you again and I feared that I had lost you for ever. You have won my heart completely and I would have you stay with me here on earth to the end of my days."

To his delight, the maiden consented:

"I will come with you, Rhiwallon," she said, "and I will remain true to you, but on one condition: if you strike me three times, three causeless blows, I must return to the place from which I came and you will lose me for ever. Now stay here a little while longer, I promise I will not keep you waiting long this time."

Letting his hand go, she slipped into the water.

Rhiwallon stood anxiously by the lakeside, he was afraid he had lost her again, but soon he saw not one but two maidens rising from the lake, accompanied by a man of noble appearance, who looked strong and youthful, although his hair was grey with age.

"Do you wish to marry one of my daughters?" asked the old man.

"If I do not, I will die," declared Rhiwallon.

"That would be a pity, for you are a fine looking young man," replied the old man. "I will be happy to give her to you, but you see that I have two daughters. Only point out to me the one you believe to be your own true love, and she shall be yours."

Rhiwallon was perplexed. The two maidens looked so much alike that he could not tell them apart. As he hesitated, one of the maidens sighed a little and imperceptibly pushed her tiny foot forward from beneath her robe. This attracted Rhiwallon's attention and he remembered seeing the way she had tied the dainty bow across her shoe as she stepped on the shore of the lake for the third time and accepted his gift of bread.

Taking her hand, he said, "This is the lady I love more than my own heart."

"You have chosen well," replied the old man. "Be to her a kind and faithful husband and I will give as her dowry, as many sheep, cattle, goats and horses as she can count, without drawing breath. But I will repeat the warning that she has already given to you. If you strike her three times without cause, you will lose her, and her dowry."

Rhiwallon earnestly gave his pledge. He did not think it would be difficult to keep such a promise. He was certain that it would be unthinkable to strike such a dainty creature.

So the maiden stood on the shore of the lake and took one deep, deep breath which was all she was allowed, and she began counting. She counted in fives as many times as possible in rapid succession, until all her breath was spent. As she counted, her father called up the animals that he had promised as her dowry.

First her father called up from the water a flock of fine looking, healthy sheep which gathered on the shores of the lake.

With the same breath, she continued to count as her father called prime, white cattle and they came up out of the lake to stand on the shore.

With the same breath, she went on counting as her father called flock of sturdy-looking goats who joined the other animals, gambolling and butting each other.

With the last of her breath, she counted as her father called a magnificent herd of horses that trotted and galloped out of the lake and stood neighing and shaking their manes close to the sheep and cattle and goats.

The maiden drew in a deep breath as she looked triumphantly at the dowry she had brought to her new husband.

She bade farewell to her father and her sister and joined hands with Rhiwallon.

Together they made their way to the small farm at Blaensawdde. Rhiwallon was the happiest of men; he had won a beautiful wife and a magnificent dowry which would bring him great wealth.

The couple, together with their cattle and other livestock, made their home on a farm called Esgair Llaethdy, a mile from the village of Myddfai, where they lived and prospered for several years. The maiden bore Rhiwallon three sons, all beautiful children.

One day, they were invited to a christening. The maiden was reluctant, and claimed that it was too far for her to travel. Rhiwallon particularly wanted

The Lady of Llyn-y-Fan Fach

to attend the christening, because they were to be the special guests of the parents.

Rhiwallon persuaded his wife, "Go and fetch one of the horses in the field, that will make the journey easier for you."

The lady turned towards the stable in obedience to her husband's request. She hesitated, "I have left my gloves in the house," she said, "will you bring them to me, as I make my way down towards the horse."

Rhiwallon went back into the house and returned with the gloves only to find that his wife was still lingering, and had made no attempt to fetch the horse. Playfully he tapped her on the shoulder with one of the gloves saying, "Hurry up, come along or we will be late!"

She looked at him sorrowfully and said, "That is the first causeless blow, husband. Remember your pledge."

Rhiwallon was chastened and silent for the rest of that day, remembering the promise he had made to her and to her father on the lakeside of Llyn-y-Fan Fach.

A few months later, Rhiwallon and his wife were invited to a wedding. The guests were making merry and thoroughly enjoying themselves when suddenly the lady burst into uncontrollable weeping. Her sobbing made the other guests turn to look at her in some surprise, and Rhiwallon touched her sharply on the shoulder, and asked her why she was so upset.

The lady looked at him sadly, "I am thinking of the troubles the couple will have to face in the coming years, and that your troubles are also beginning. You know, husband," she said, "that is the second blow. If you strike me once more, you will lose me for ever."

Rhiwallon was so despondent that he hid his face in his hands and wept. He vowed that he would be very careful in future, for he loved his wife dearly and did not wish to lose her.

Years passed, and the three sons grew up to become strong, fine men, and they proved to be particularly clever. Life was good and Rhiwallon began to forget that there remained only one causeless blow which would destroy his happiness and prosperity.

Rhiwallon's mother died. Rhiwallon was heartbroken, for he had loved his mother very much. At the funeral, he could not control his tears and heartache. As he and his wife knelt together in their pew in church, he heard a sound from his wife. Through his tears he looked at her and could not believe his eyes. She was smiling and chuckling to herself; she looked as happy as if they were attending a wedding party! Rhiwallon was shocked. He touched her on the shoulder:

"Hush, hush, dear," he said, "please don't laugh like that."

"I laugh," she said, "because when people die, they go out of trouble." She paused and looked sorrowfully at her husband.

"The last blow has been struck," she said, "our marriage contract is at an end."

So saying, she set off for Esgair Llaethdy where she called the cattle and other livestock together.

First, she called the cows, and they came to her from the barns and the cowsheds and the fields where they were grazing. Then she called the sheep,

Lake Stories of Wales

and they came running and leaping from the green fields and the mountain slopes. Then she called the goats, and they came jumping from the rocks and running from the bushes. Then she called the horses, and they came to her trotting and whinnying. When she had gathered all the creatures in this fashion, they followed her across the Black Mountain, towards the lake from whence they came, a distance of more than six miles. They disappeared into the water and the waters closed over them until not a trace remained of the maiden or the animals.

Rhiwallon was demented with grief. The woman he loved more than life itself, was gone from him for ever. He rushed down to the lakeside and, in his anguish, he flung himself into the water. He was never seen again.

After this distressing event, the three sons often wandered near the lake hoping that their mother may be permitted to re-appear once more. Their father had often told them the story of their mother's mysterious origin, and of how she had appeared to him and brought with her the dowry of cattle and livestock from the lake.

One day, the three sons were walking near Dôl Howel at the Mountain Gate, now called the Physicians Gate. Their mother appeared and approached her eldest son.

"My dearest son," she said, "take this as my love and my blessing." She offered him a wallet which he took from her in wonder and silence. He put his hand inside and drew out a parchment on which was inscribed many verses containing remedies for healing people from sickness and disease.

"It is my gift to you and it is my promise that you and your children will become the most skilful of physicians for many generations to come."

She left him to ponder on her words and her prophesy, but she returned on several occasions to walk and talk with him and with his brothers.

Once she even accompanied them home as far as a place now called Pant y Meddygon (the Dingle of the Physician), where she pointed out to them the plants and herbs which grew in the dingle and explained their medicinal qualities.

It is said that the three sons became physicians to Rhys Grug, Lord of Llandovery and Dinefwr Castle, who gave them lands and privileges at Myddfai. This enabled the sons of Rhiwallon and the Lady of the Lake to give the best medical advice and treatment free to anyone in need, whatever their rank or means.

The sons became unrivalled in their reputation as physicians and became celebrated throughout the land. They wisely committed their knowledge to writing, so that it may be of benefit to future generations.

If you visit Myddfai today, the inhabitants will be eager to tell you the story of the Lady of the Lake and her sons, still known as The Physicians of Myddfai.